T0046607

THE ROAD TO THE CITY

STORYBOOK ND
CURATED BY GINI ALHADEFF

César Aira, *The Famous Magician*

Osamu Dazai, *Early Light*

Helen DeWitt, *The English Understand Wool*

Natalia Ginzburg, *The Road to the City*

Rachel Ingalls, *In the Act*

László Krasznahorkai, *Spadework for a Palace*

Clarice Lispector, *The Woman Who Killed the Fish*

Yoko Tawada, *Three Streets*

THE ROAD TO THE CITY
NATALIA GINZBURG

translated from the Italian
by Gini Alhadeff

STORYBOOK ND

Originally published in Italian as *La strada che va in città* in 1942, under the pseudonym Alessandra Tornimparte. Published by arrangement with Einaudi Edizioni

Publisher's Note: The epigraph is from Ecclesiastes 10:15. The afterword was originally an introduction by Natalia Ginzburg to *Cinque romanzi brevi* (Einaudi, 1964)

Manufactured in the United States of America
First published clothbound by New Directions in 2023

Library of Congress Cataloging-in-Publication Data
Names: Ginzburg, Natalia, author. | Alhadeff, Gini, translator.
Title: The road to the city / Natalia Ginzburg ;
translated from the Italian by Gini Alhadeff.
Other titles: Strada che va in città. English
Description: New York : New Directions Books, 2023.
Identifiers: LCCN 2023001736 | ISBN 9780811234757 (hardcover ; acid-free paper) | ISBN 9780811234764 (ebook)
Subjects: LCGFT: Novellas.
Classification: LCC PQ4817.I5 S713 2023 |
DDC 853/.912—dc23/eng/20230201
LC record available at https://lccn.loc.gov/2023001736

10 9 8 7 6 5 4 3 2 1

New Directions Books are published for James Laughlin
by New Directions Publishing Corporation
80 Eighth Avenue, NY 10011

THE ROAD TO THE CITY

"The labor of fools will be their torment, since they don't know the road to the city."

Nini had been living with us since he was little. He was the son of a cousin of my father's. His parents had died and he was supposed to live with his grandfather, but his grandfather would hit him with a broom so he'd run away and come to us. But then the grandfather died and that's when they told him that from now on he could stay with us.

Not counting Nini, there were five of us. Before me was my sister Azalea, who was married and lived in the city. My brother Giovanni came after me, then came Gabriele and Vittorio. They say that a house with many children is full of joy, but I didn't think there was anything joyful about our house. I hoped to get married soon and to get away as my sister Azalea had done. Azalea had married at the age of seventeen. I was sixteen but no one had asked me yet. Giovanni and Nini also wanted to leave home. Only the little ones were still content.

Our house was a red house, with a pergola in front. We kept our clothes on the stair railings because there were many of us and not enough closets. "*Shoo, shoo,*" my mother would say, chasing the chickens out of the kitchen, "*shoo, shoo* ..." The gramophone played all day long and since we had only one record, the song was always the same. It sang:

Velvety hands
Sweet-smelling hands
An old-fashioned thrill
I can't explain

That song where the words had such strange inflections appealed to every one of us, and all day long we repeated it, as we got up, and as we went to bed. Giovanni and Nini slept in the room next to mine and in the morning they would wake me up by banging on the wall three times: I would dress quickly and off we went to the city. The trip took about an hour. The moment we reached town we parted like three perfect strangers. I would look for a friend and go strolling beneath the porticoes. Sometimes I'd run into Azalea, her nose red beneath the veil of her hat, and she wouldn't greet me because I didn't have a hat on.

I ate bread and oranges by the river, with my friend, or I'd go to Azalea's. I nearly always found her in bed, reading novels, or smoking, or phoning her lover, quarreling because she was jealous, caring not at all that the children might hear. Then her husband came home and she quarreled with him too. Her husband was already quite old, with a beard and glasses. He paid hardly any attention to her but read the newspaper, sighing, and scratching his head. "God help me," he'd mutter to himself every now and then. Ottavia, the fourteen-year-old maid with a matted black plait down her back, and a little child in her arms, would stand by the door saying, "The Signora is served." Azalea would slip on some stockings, yawn, gaze at her legs for a long spell, and then we would go to the table. When the phone rang Azalea would blush, crush her napkin, and Ottavia's voice in the next room could be heard saying, "The Signora is busy, she will call back later." After lunch the husband would go out again, and Azalea would get back into bed and fall asleep instantly. Her face then became tender and calm. All the while, the phone rang, doors slammed, the children yelled, but Azalea went on sleeping, breathing deeply. Ottavia cleared the table and asked, quaking, what might happen if the "Signore" were ever to find out. But then she would whisper, smiling bitterly, that after all the "Signore" also had someone. I left. I waited for nightfall on a bench in the public gardens. The café orchestra played and my friend and I looked at the dresses on women passing by, and I would also see Nini and Giovanni going by, but we never spoke. I'd meet them again outside the city, on the dusty road, as houses lit up behind us and the café orchestra grew louder and played more boisterously. We walked through the countryside, by the river and the trees. We'd reach home. I hated our house. I hated the green and bitter soup our mother placed before us every evening and I hated our mother. I would have been ashamed of her if I'd come across her in the city. But it was many years since she'd been to the city, and she looked like a peasant. Her hair was disheveled and gray, and her front teeth were missing. "You look like a witch, Mammà," Azalea would say when she came home. "Why don't you get dentures?" Then she would stretch out on the red sofa in the dining room, kick off her shoes and say, "Coffee!" She quickly drank the coffee my mother brought her, slept a little, then left. My mother said that children are like poison and should never be brought into the world. She spent her days cursing all of her children, one by one. When my mother was young a court clerk had fallen in love with her and taken her to Milan. My mother had stayed there a few days, but then she had come back. She told the story repeatedly, saying she'd gone away because she was tired of the children, and, as for the court clerk, they'd invented him. "I wish I'd never come back," my mother would say, with her fingers mopping her tears all over her face. My mother never stopped talking, but I never answered. No one ever answered her. Only Nini answered her every now and then. He was not like us, though we had grown up together. Though we were cousins he did not resemble us. His face was pale, and never tanned even after being out in the sun, and he had a lock of hair that fell over his eyes. In his pockets he always carried newspapers and books—he read all the time, he even read while eating and Giovanni would turn his book upside down to spite him. Nini would pick it up and go on reading calmly, running his fingers through the lock of hair. Meanwhile, the record player repeated,

Velvety hands
Sweet-smelling hands

The little children played and hit one another and my mother would come to slap them, then she would take it out on me for sitting on the sofa instead of helping her with the dishes. My father would then tell her that she should be bringing me up better. My mother would start sobbing, saying that she was everyone's dog, and my father would take his hat off the coat rack and go out. My father worked as an electrician and a photographer, and he wanted Giovanni to train to be an electrician. But Giovanni never went when he was called. There was never enough money and my father was always tired and furious. He'd come home briefly and then leave right away because the house was a madhouse, he said. But he'd say that it wasn't our fault if we were so badly brought up. That it was his fault and my mother's. By the look of him my father still seemed quite young and my mother was jealous. He washed thoroughly before dressing, and put brilliantine in his hair. I was not ashamed of him when I ran into him in town. Nini also liked to wash, and he stole my father's brilliantine. But it was no use as the lock of hair would bounce back over his eyes all the same.

Once Giovanni told me: "Nini drinks grappa."

I stared at him, surprised.

"Grappa? Always?"

"Whenever he can," he said, "any chance he gets. He even took a bottle of it home. And keeps it hidden. But I found it and he let me taste it. It's good," he said.

"Nini drinks grappa," I repeated to myself in amazement. I went to Azalea's. I found her at home alone. She was sitting at the table in the kitchen. And eating tomato salad with a vinegar dressing.

"Nini drinks grappa," I told her.

She shrugged.

"You have to find something to do, to fight the boredom."

"Yes, one gets bored. Why are we so bored?" I asked.

"Because life is stupid," she said, pushing her plate away. "What can you do? You get tired of everything right away."

"Why are we always so bored?" I asked Nini that evening, as we walked home.

"Who's bored? I'm not bored at all," he said and started laughing, taking me by the arm. "So you're bored? But why? Everything is so wonderful."

"What's so wonderful?" I asked.

"Everything," he said, "everything. I like everything I see. A little while ago I liked walking in the city, now I am walking in the countryside and I like that, too. "

Giovanni was walking just ahead of us. He stopped and said:

"He goes to work in a factory now."

"I am learning to be a lathe turner," Nini said, "so I'll have some money. I can't be without money. I can't stand it. All I need to cheer me up is a few lira in my pocket. But when you want money you have to either steal it or earn it. They never properly explained that to us at home. They always complain about us, but just to pass the time. No one ever said, 'Get out, and shut up!' That's what they should have done.

"If they'd told me 'Get out, and shut up,' I would have kicked them out the door," Giovanni said.

On the way, we met the doctor's son, who had gone hunting with his dog. He had shot down seven or eight quails, and gave me two. He was a stocky young man, with a big black mustache, who was at the university studying medicine. He and Nini started arguing, and later Giovanni told me:

"The doctor's son is no match for Nini. Nini isn't like the others, and it doesn't matter that he hasn't studied."

But I was happy because Giulio had given me two quails, and he'd looked at me and said that one day we should go to the city together.

Summer had come now, and I started thinking of my clothes and that I should get new ones made. I told my mother I needed some light blue fabric, and my mother asked if I thought she had millions in her purse, but I said I also needed a pair of shoes with cork soles and couldn't do without them, then added, "And damn the mother who gave birth to you."

I got slapped and cried all day long locked up in my room. I asked Azalea for the money, and she sent me to Via Genova 20 to ask if Alberto was at home. Having found out that he wasn't, I went back with the answer and got the money. I stayed in my room a few days sewing, and almost forgot what the city was like. Once the dress was finished I put it on and went for a walk, and the doctor's son came up to me right away, bought some pastries and we went to eat them under the pine trees. He asked me what I'd been doing locked up at home all that time. But I told him I didn't like people meddling in my business. He begged me not to be so mean. Then he tried to kiss me but I got away.

I lay out all morning on the balcony at home, to tan my legs in the sun. I had the shoes with cork soles and I had the dress, and I also had a woven straw handbag Azalea had given me in return for taking a letter to Via Genova 20. And my face, legs, and arms had taken on a nice brown color. Someone came to tell my mother that Giulio, the doctor's son, was in love with me and that his mother had berated him for hours about it. My mother suddenly became all cheerful and sweet, and every morning brought me a beaten egg yolk because she thought I was looking a bit out of sorts. The doctor's wife spent all day long at the window with the maid, and when she caught sight of me banged the window shut as though she'd seen a serpent. Giulio gave me a half smile and went on walking next to me and talking. I didn't pay any attention to what he was saying—I was thinking that this stocky young man with the black mustache, and high boots, who whistled to summon his dog, would soon be my boyfriend, and that many girls in town would weep with rage.

Giovanni came to tell me, "Azalea is asking for you." I hadn't been to the city for quite some time. I went wearing my light blue dress, and the shoes, with the handbag and my sunglasses. At Azalea's everything was upside down, the beds hadn't been made, and Ottavia was leaning against the wall, sobbing, with the children hanging on to her skirts.

"He left her," she told me, "he's getting married."

Azalea sat on the bed in her slip, her eyes wide and glistening. A sheaf of letters rested on her lap.

"He is getting married in September," she said.

"We have to hide everything now, before the Signore gets back," said Ottavia, gathering up the letters.

"No, we must burn them," said Azalea, "Burn them! I never want to see them again. I never want to see that face again. That mean stupid face," she said tearing up the photo of a smiling officer. And she began to cry and shout, hitting her head against the headboard.

"She is going to have convulsions now, "said Ottavia, "that's how it was with my mother sometimes. We should put some cold water on her belly."

Azalea did not allow us to bathe her stomach with cold water, and said that she wanted to be left alone and that we should go call her husband because she wanted to confess everything. It was hard to convince Azalea not to call anyone. We burnt the letters on the kitchen stove while Ottavia read bits of them to me before throwing them into the fire, and the children chased the burning bits of paper all over the room. When Azalea's husband came home I told him that Azalea was ill and had a fever, and he went to get a doctor.

When I got home it was night and my father asked where I'd been. I said that Azalea had called me, and Giovanni told him that was true. My father said this might be so but that he had been told I was running around with the doctor's son and if that was true he'd smash my face. I said I didn't care and would do as I pleased, but then I had a fit of rage and knocked over the soup which spilled all over the floor. I locked myself up in my room for two or three hours, crying, till Giovanni shouted to me through the wall to shut up and let them all sleep, since everyone was tired. But I went on crying and Nini came to the door saying that if I opened it he'd give me some chocolate. I opened the door and Nini took me to the mirror so that I might see my swollen face, and really did give me some chocolate, and told me that his girlfriend had given it to him. I asked what the girlfriend was like and why he hadn't shown her to me, and he told me that she had wings, and a tail, and wore a carnation in her hair. I told him I had a boyfriend who was the son of the doctor, and he said, "Excellent," but then made a strange face and got up to leave. So I asked him where he had hidden the grappa. He went red in the face and laughed, and said that these were not things that a young girl should concern herself with.

The next evening Nini did not come home. He didn't do so even in the days that followed. Nini's face was no longer to be seen, to the point that even my father, who was always so absentminded, noticed and asked where on earth he could be. Giovanni replied that he was all right but that he wouldn't be coming home for the time being.

My father said:

"They come when they feel like it, then they find something better and goodbye. Children or not children, they're all alike."

But Giovanni later told me that Nini was now with his girlfriend, and that she was a widow, but young, and that her name was Antonietta.

So I went to the city to look for Nini and to find out if all that was true. I found him at the café with Giovanni, and they were having ice cream. I sat down and had ice cream with them, and we stayed there some time listening to music, and Nini like a gentleman paid for everyone. I asked him if it was true about the widow. He said yes, that it was true, and why didn't I pay him a visit at the small apartment where he lived with Antonietta and her two children, a boy and a girl. And he also said that Antonietta had a store that sold stationery and fountain pens and that she was quite well off.

"So you are going to be a kept man," I said.

"A kept man? Why? I am earning money." And he told me he had a decent salary working at the factory and that he was planning to send some money home soon.

I told Giulio about Nini while we smoked in the woods, and I said I'd go pay him a visit one day.

17

"You mustn't go," he said.

"Why?"

"There are things you can't understand, you are still a child."

I replied that I was not a child at all, that I was seventeen and my sister Azalea had gotten married at seventeen. But he repeated that I couldn't understand and that a young girl should not go to a house where a man and a woman were living together without being married. I went home in a bad mood that evening and as I undressed to go to bed I thought that Giulio was taking me to the woods and was having a good time kissing me, and time was going by and he hadn't asked me yet. And I was in a rush to get married. But I was thinking that after getting married I wanted to be free to have a great time, and maybe with Giulio I wouldn't be free at all. Maybe he would do what his father had done, when he had locked his own wife up at home, saying that a woman's place is within the walls of her own home, and she had become a bitter old woman who spent all day at the window watching people go by.

I couldn't say why but it seemed to me very bad not to see Nini around the house, with the lock of hair over his eyes, and his old raincoat coming undone, and his books, and not to hear him preach that I should help my mother. One day I went to see him to spite Giulio. It was a Sunday, and they made tea for me with pastries on a beautiful embroidered tablecloth, and Antonietta, who was the widow, welcomed me and kissed me on both cheeks. She was a well dressed little woman, made up, with fluffy blond hair, narrow shoulders and a thick waist. The children were also there doing their homework. Nini sat by the radio, and didn't always have a book in his hand as he did at home. They showed me the whole apartment. There was a bathroom, the master bedroom, and small pots of succulent plants everywhere. The place was much more clean and sparkling than Azalea's. We talked about one thing and another, and they invited me to come back often.

Nini walked with me part of the way back. I asked him why he no longer came home, and told him that without him I was more bored than ever at home. And I wanted to cry. He sat next to me on a bench and held me tight a little, and as he did so stroked my hands and told me to stop crying or the black makeup around my eyes would melt. I told him I didn't put black around my eyes and that I wasn't like Antonietta, who looked like a clown all made up like that, and that he'd be better off coming home. But he said I should look for a job and come live in the city, because then we could got to the movies together at night, but that I had to do something to earn some money and be independent. I told him I had no intention of doing anything of the sort and he should put it out of his mind, and that soon I would marry Giulio and we would come live in the city, because Giulio didn't like our town either. That's how we parted.

I told Giulio that I'd been to see Nini, but he didn't get angry. He only said he was sorry that I did things that upset him. I told him about Antonietta and about the apartment, and he asked me if I'd like to have an apartment like hers. Then he said that as soon as he passed his state medical exams, we would get married, that before that it wouldn't be possible, and in the meantime I shouldn't be so mean.

"I'm not mean," I said.

He told me to go the next day to Fonte Le Macchie with him. To get to Fonte Le Macchie you had to walk uphill part of the way and I didn't like walking uphill, and what's more, I was scared of vipers.

"There are no vipers around there," he said, "and we can eat blackberries and rest any time you please."

For a time I pretended not to understand and I told him that Giovanni would come with us but he said that he didn't want Giovanni to come and that it had to be just the two of us.

We never made it to Fonte Le Macchie because I stopped, sat on a rock and told him I wasn't going any further. To scare me he started shouting that he could see a viper, yes, yes, he had seen it, it was yellow and was swinging its tail this way and that. I told him to leave me alone because I was dead tired and hungry, too. He took some food out of the bag. He also had some wine in a flask and made me drink some, till I lay down in the grass dazed and what I'd been expecting happened.

When we started back down it was late, but I was so tired I had to stop at every other step, so that when we reached the end of the woods he said he had to run ahead because otherwise he would be late and his mother worried. And so he left me alone and I walked stumbling over every stone, and it was getting dark and my knees hurt.

The next day Azalea came home. I walked back with her some of the way and told her how it had been. She didn't believe me at first and thought I was just bragging, but all of a sudden she stopped and said:

"Is it true?"

"It's true, it's true, Azalea," I said, then she asked me to repeat it all, from the beginning. She was so afraid and worried that she tore the buckle off her belt. She wanted to tell her husband so that he might let our father know. I told her that on no account should she do so and that I knew some fine things about her I could tell, too. We argued and the next day I went into the city just to make up with her, but when I got there she had calmed down and was trying on a new dance outfit since she had received an invitation. She told me to do whatever the hell I pleased as long as no one came to bug her, and what's more, she didn't like the doctor's son at all—she thought him very coarse. On my way back I saw Giovanni with Nini and Antonietta and we all went for a swim in the river, except for Antonietta who couldn't swim and stayed on the boat. I hung on to the side of the boat as though to capsize it just to frighten her, but then I was feeling cold, so I got back on the boat and started rowing. Antonietta started telling me about her husband and his illness, of the debts he'd left and the lawyers and the lawsuits. I was bored and thought she looked funny, sitting in the boat with her knees pressed together and her hat and handbag, as though on a formal visit.

That night Giovanni came to my room to tell me that he had fallen in love with Antonietta, and didn't know whether he should tell Nini, or what he should do to get over it, and he walked up and down with his hands in his pockets. But I was tough on him, I told him I was sick of all those love stories, of Azalea, and Nini, and of him, too, and couldn't they all please just leave me alone. "Damn the mother that brought you into the world," he said and left slamming the door behind him.

Giulio told me it was with him that I should go swim in the river, and to the city, too—that I should go with him so we could have a good time, both of us together. So I did go and we swam in the river and had ice cream, then he would take me to a room in a hotel he knew. The hotel was called Le Lune: it was at the end of an old street, and with its shutters drawn and deserted little garden, it gave the impression of an abandoned villa. But the rooms had a sink, a mirror, and rugs on the floor. I would tell Azalea that we'd been to the hotel, and she would say that sooner or later I'd get into trouble. But I wasn't seeing much of Azalea now because she had another lover, a penniless student for whom she was constantly buying gloves and shoes and things to eat.

One evening my father came to my room, flung his raincoat on the bed, saying, "I told you I'd smash your face."

He grabbed me by my hair and started slapping me, while I yelled, "Help! Help!" till my mother came, all out of breath, with potatoes in her apron, and asked:

"What happened? What are you doing to her, Attilio?"

My father said:

"Of all the things we had to witness, poor wretches that we are," and he sat down, his face pale, running his hands through his hair. My lip was bleeding, and I had red welts on my neck, I was dizzy and almost couldn't stand up, and my mother wanted to help me staunch the blood, but my father grabbed her by one arm and pushed her out. He left, too, and I was by myself. My father's raincoat was still on the bed, so I took it and flung it down the stairs. While they were all having dinner, I went out. It was a clear and starry night. I trembled from shock and from the cold, and my lip was still bleeding. I had blood on my dress, even on my stockings. I took the road to the city. I didn't really know where I was going. At first I thought I'd go to Azalea's, but her husband would be there and he'd start asking questions and preaching. So I went to Nini's instead. I found them sitting around the dining-room table playing a board game called *gioco dell'oca*. They looked at me in shock and the children started screaming. I threw myself on the couch and started to cry. Antonietta brought a disinfectant for my lip, then she had me drink a cup of chamomile tea and they made up a cot for me in the hall. Nini said:

"Tell us what happened, Delia."

I told him that my father had lunged at me and wanted to kill me because I was going out with Giulio, and that they should find me a job so that I could come to the city, because I couldn't live at home any more.

Nini said:

"Just take your clothes off now and get into bed, then I'll come back and we'll think what's to be done."

Everyone left and I undressed and slipped into bed, wearing a pale lilac shirt Antonietta had lent me. After a while Nini came back, sat next to my bed, and said:

"If you like, I'll try to get you a job at the factory where I work. You'll find it hard to begin with, because you're all grown up and never learned to do a single thing. But you'll get used to it little by little. If I can't find anything at the factory you'll have to find work as a domestic."

I said I didn't want to work as a domestic and preferred to work in a factory, and asked him why I couldn't be a flower girl, sitting on the steps of a church with baskets of flowers. He said:

"Shush now and don't be silly. Besides, you couldn't sell anything because you can't even add and subtract."

I told him Giulio was going to marry me after passing his state medical exams.

"Forget it," he said.

And he told me that Giulio had a girlfriend in the city, and that the whole city knew about it: a thin woman who drove a car. I started to cry again and Nini told me to lie down and sleep, and he brought me another pillow so that I could be comfortable.

The next morning I dressed and went out with him. The city was fresh and deserted. He walked with me to the outskirts of the city. We sat by the river and waited till it was time for him to go to work. He told me that sometimes he felt like going to Milan to look for work in some large factory.

"But first you'd have to get rid of Antonietta."

"Of course. You wouldn't want me to take her with me along with the shop and the two brats."

25

"You don't love her then," I said.

"I love her like this: we stay together as long as it pleases us, then we break up and leave each other in peace, and good day."

" Let Giovanni have her then—he's crazy about her," I said, and he started to laugh.

"Oh Giovanni? After all Antonietta is not that bad, she is a bit squeamish but not a mean sort. Still, I am not in love."

"Who are you in love with?" I asked and it suddenly occurred to me that he might be in love with me.

Laughing, he looked at me and said: "Does one have to be in love with someone? It's possible not to love any-one and to be interested in something else altogether."

My teeth were chattering from the cold in my light dress.

"You are cold, darling," he said. He took off his jacket and dropped it on my shoulders.

I said: "How tender you are."

"Why shouldn't I be tender with you," he said, "you are so wretched I feel sorry for you. You think I don't know that you've gotten yourself into a real bind with that Giulio. I've guessed it because I know you ,and Azalea told me so, too."

"That's not true," I said, but he replied that I had better shut up because he knew me and he wasn't that dumb.

The sirens sounded and Nini said he had to go to work. He wanted me to keep his jacket, but I refused because I was afraid of running into someone and felt funny wearing a man's jacket. We said goodbye and I said:

"But Nini, why don't you ever come home any more?"

And so he promised to come see me the next day which was a Sunday. Then he bent down quickly and kissed me on one cheek. I stood still and watched him as he went away, with his hands in his pockets and his steady step. I was still totally dazed that he'd kissed me. He'd never done that. I started walking very slowly all the while thinking about Nini who had kissed me and a little bit about Giulio who had a girlfriend in the city and had hidden it from me, and I thought: "How strange people are. One never knows what they are going to do." And then I thought that at home I'd be seeing my father again and that maybe he'd hit me again, and I felt sad.

But my father didn't say a word and behaved as though I wasn't there, and the others did the same. Only my mother brought me some coffee with milk and asked me where I'd been. I didn't see Giulio in town and I didn't know where he was, whether out hunting or in the city.

The next day Nini came all excited and happy, and told me that he'd found me a job, not at the factory because there they'd turned him down right away, but there was an old slightly unhinged lady who needed someone to go out with her in the afternoon. I would have to be in the city every day right after lunch and would go back home in the evening. To start, the pay was meager and wouldn't allow me to live alone in the city, but then she would no doubt increase it, Nini promised. That lady was an acquaintance of Antonietta's and she had been the one to recommend me. There was no one at home that day and Nini and I stayed by ourselves the whole time. We stretched out under the pergola and we were able to talk in peace as if we were by the river.

"But it was nicer by the river," he told me. "Come again in the morning by the river and we'll bathe, too. You have no idea how wonderful it is to swim early in the morning. It's not cold and one feels revived."

But again I started asking him who he was in love with.

"Leave me alone," he said, "let me be and don't torment me today—I am so happy."

"Tell me Nini," I said, "tell me, and I promise not to tell anyone."

"What do you care?" he said and started to tell me how I should wash properly and wear a dark dress to go meet the old lady. I answered that I didn't have a dark dress and that if it was going to be that complicated I didn't feel like going any more. Then he got cross and left without even saying goodbye.

I went to the old lady's wearing my usual light blue dress. She was waiting for me, ready to go out, all dressed, wearing a hat, her face powdered. I was to walk with her and entertain her—so her daughter told me—then take her home and read the newspaper to her out loud till she fell asleep. I took short steps, with her hand slipped through my arm. The old lady did nothing but complain. She said I was too tall and that holding on to my arm tired her. She said I walked too quickly. She had a holy terror of crossing the street, and would start to moan and tremble so that everyone turned around to look at her. One time we ran into Azalea. She didn't know yet that I was working and stared at me dumbfounded.

Once back at her house the old lady drank a cup of milk the way old people do while I read the newspaper to her. After a while she'd start falling asleep and I'd take off. But I was in a bad mood and couldn't take pleasure in either the city or the shops. One evening I decided to go meet Nini at the factory. He saw me from a distance and his entire face lit up. But when I saw him up close—wearing an old hat that was too light, shoes that were worn out and too wide so that he dragged his feet, and looking dirty and tired—I regretted having come to pick him up and was ashamed for him. He saw what I was thinking and was offended, and got angry at me because I said I was bored stiff with the old lady.

But when we reached the river he brightened little by little, and started to tell me that in Antonietta's drawer he had found a photo of Giovanni, dedicated at the back.

"So much the better," he said.

"So much the better? Why so much the better?"

"What the hell do you think I care?"

"You're a cold fish. You make me sick."

"So I'm a fish. So what? And what about you?" He looked at me for a while then said: "You're a poor girl."

"Why?"

"Is it true that you agreed to go to Le Lune?"

"Who told you?"

"My little finger told me," he said. "You went there more than once didn't you?"

"It's none of your business."

"Poor girl! Poor girl!" he repeated as though to himself.

I got angry and covered his mouth with my hand. Then he put his arms around me and drew me down to the ground, where I lay sprawled, and he kissed my face, kissed my ears, my hair.

"Have you gone mad, Nini? What are you doing to me?" I was saying, and part of me wanted to laugh and another part was a bit scared.

He got up, smoothing his hair, and said:

"See what you are? Anyone can have all the fun they want with you."

"And what—now you wanted to find out if it's as you say?"

"No. Never mind. I was only kidding," he said.

*

Giulio was waiting for me on the street that evening.

"Where have you been all this time?" I asked him.

"In bed with a fever," he said, and tried to take my arm. But I told him to go away and leave me alone, because I knew he had a girlfriend.

"What girlfriend? Who?"

"One who has a car."

He started laughing out loud, slapping his knee.

"They make up any old story," he said, "and you just fall for it. Don't be silly and meet me in the woods tomorrow after lunch."

But I said I was no longer free in the afternoon and told him about the old lady.

"Come in the morning, then," he said.

I turned my head away and didn't want to let him look at me for fear he would guess that Nini had kissed me.

The next morning in the woods he wouldn't stop trying to find out who had told me about the girlfriend.

"I have many enemies," he said, "there's so much envy in the world."

He pestered me so much I finally told him it was Nini.

"If I see Nini I'll give him a piece of my mind," he told me. Then he started to tease me about taking the old lady out for walks, just to bug me.

I went to get Nini at the factory again. But he was cross with me because at the old lady's house they had complained to Antonietta that I was always late.

"One can never count on you," he said. "Keep it up and you'll go very far. A good thing they didn't take you on at the factory."

I told him I was sick of the old lady and wouldn't go there any more.

"At least go there till the end of the month, so that you get paid. Then give the money to your mother because the little ones will be needing shoes."

"I'm keeping the money for myself," I said.

"Good for you, that's perfect. Think only of yourself. Buy some rag you can put on, and have fun. I don't care anyway."

He refused to go to the river, and started walking towards his house. We found Antonietta as she was closing the store. She was very angry and said that if she'd known how I was she would never have recommended me. How bad I'd made her look. I was forever late getting to the old lady's and left much too early, and when I read the newspaper to her I kept laughing and getting the words wrong on purpose. She hardly said goodbye and left with Nini. On the way home I felt tired and sad. I hadn't been feeling well for some days, I felt a kind of queasiness and couldn't eat any more—even the smell of food made me sick. "What's the matter with me? Maybe I'm pregnant," I thought. "What will I do now?" I stopped. The countryside was quiet around me and I could no longer see the city, I couldn't see our house yet and I was alone on the empty road, with that fright in my heart. There were girls going to school, they were going to the beach in the summer, they danced, and kidded around among themselves. Why wasn't I with them? Why wasn't my life like that?

When I reached my room, I lit a cigarette. But that cigarette tasted bad. I remembered that Azalea too couldn't smoke while expecting her children. That was happening to me now. I was pregnant for sure. When my father found out, he'd kill me. "So much the better," I thought, "to die. To end it forever."

But in the morning I woke up calmer. The sun was out. I went to pick some grapes from the arbor with the little kids. I walked around town with Giulio. There was a fair and he bought me a good-luck charm to hang around my neck. Every now and then that fright came over me, but I pushed it away. I did not tell him anything. I had fun being at the fair, with people shouting, the chickens in wooden cages, and kids playing little trumpets. I remembered that Nini was cross with me and decided I would go find him the next day to make peace.

It was a holiday that day and I didn't have to go to the old lady. Nini did not have to go to the factory. I found him just as he was leaving the café. He wasn't angry any more and asked if I wanted to have something. I said I didn't and we went to the river.

"Let's make peace," I said after we sat down.

"Let's by all means make peace. But in a little while I have to go to Antonietta's."

"Can't I come, too? Is Antonietta still very angry?"

"Yes. She says you never thanked her for all that she did for you. And she's jealous too."

"Jealous of me?"

"Yes, you."

"How happy that makes me."

"Of course that makes you happy, ugly monkey that you are. You really love making people suffer. And I really have to go now. But I don't feel like it." He was lying on the grass, his arms folded beneath his head.

"Do you like being with me? More than with Antonietta?"

"Much more," he told me, "much much more."

"Why?"

"I don't know why. That's just how it is."

"And I like being with you. More than with anyone else," I said.

"More with me than with Giulio?"

"More with you."

"How can that be?" he said and laughed.

"I really don't know," I said. I wondered whether he would kiss me again. But so many people were going by that day. All at once I saw Giovanni and Antonietta coming toward us.

"I was certain I'd find them here," Giovanni cried. But Antonietta gave me a cold cold look and didn't speak to me. Nini got up limply and we went walking with them around the city.

That evening Giovanni told me:

"What a strange kid you are. Now you have this thing for Nini and you're always with Nini, practically stitched to Nini—you can always be found with him."

It was true that I was always with Nini. I went to

fetch him every evening at the factory. I couldn't wait for the moment when I'd be with him. I liked being with him. When we were together, I'd forget what I was afraid of. I liked when he talked, and I liked when he remained silent and chewed his nails while thinking about something. I kept wondering whether he would kiss me, but he didn't kiss me. He sat a little way from me and ruffled his lock of hair and smoothed it back down, and said:

"Go on home now."

But I didn't feel like going home. I was never bored when we were together. I liked it when he talked about the books he was always reading. I didn't understand what he was saying, but I pretended to understand and nodded.

"I bet you can't understand any of it," he said and gave me a light slap on the face.

One evening I felt ill just as I was undressing. I had to lie down on my bed and wait for it to pass. I was drenched in sweat and shivered. "It was like that for Azalea, too," I recalled. "Tomorrow I'll tell Giulio. He should know, after all," I thought. "But then what will we do? What will he do? Can it really be true?" But I knew for sure that it was. I couldn't sleep, flung off the covers, and sat upright in bed my heart beating. What would Nini say when he found out? At one point I had almost told him, but then was ashamed.

I found Giulio in town the next morning. He stayed with me only a moment as he had to go hunting with his father.

"You don't look well," he said.

"That's because I didn't sleep," I said.

"I hope to catch a nice hare," he told me. "I really feel like giving my feet some exercise in the woods."

He looked up at the clouds moving slowly toward the hill.

"It's a weather for hares," he said.

I didn't go to the old lady that day. After wandering around the city by myself, I went up to Azalea's. But she was out. Ottavia was there, ironing in the kitchen. Her apron was white in front, and she was not wearing slippers. Everything was different in that house when things were going well for Azalea. Even the children seemed to have gained weight. Ottavia told me, as she ironed one of Azalea's bras, that now everything was going well and Azalea was always happy. This student was not like the other man. He never forgot to call. He always did as Azalea wanted and hadn't even gone to see his parents who lived outside the city because Azalea hadn't let him. The only thing was to make sure the "Signore "didn't find out. They had to be very careful. She begged me to wait for Azalea to get back so I could tell her to be careful.

I waited awhile, but Azalea didn't come and I left. That was the hour when Nini left the factory. But I started walking home slowly. It was raining. I got home drenched and immediately got into bed, burying my face in the sheets. I told my mother I wasn't feeling well and that I didn't want to eat.

"You must have caught cold," my mother said.

The next day she came into my room, touched my face and said I didn't have a fever. And she told me to get up and help her wash the stairs.

"I can't get up," I said, "I don't feel well."

"So that's what you're playing at," she said, "you're playing at being sick. I'm the one who is going to get sick, working as I do morning and night, busting my arms for you all. When I pick up my plate I can't even eat I'm so tired. And you enjoy watching me die.

"I can't get up, I told you, I am sick."

"Well, what is it?" my mother said, tugging at the sheet so as to look at my face. "Has anything happened?"

"I am pregnant," I said. My heart was beating fast and for the first time I realized I was afraid of what my mother might do. But she was not surprised. She sat on the bed quietly, and drew the blanket over my feet.

"Are you quite sure?" she asked.

I nodded, and cried.

"Don't cry," my mother said, "you'll see it will all turn out right. Does the young man know?"

I shook my head.

"You have to tell him, damn it. But now we'll fix everything properly. I myself will go talk to those scoundrels. We'll tell them how we see it." She covered her head with the shawl and left. When she came back she seemed very satisfied, and her face was red.

"What scoundrels," she said, "but it's done. We'll just have to wait a while. The young man has to take his exams first. That was their wish. Now Attilio has to keep calm. But I'll take care of that. Your mother will take care of it. You stay in bed, nice and warm," and she brought me a cup of coffee. Then she took the pail and went to wash the stairs and I could hear her laughing to herself. But soon she was back.

"I like that young man," she said, "it's the mother I can't stand. The father immediately agreed, he said he was ready to make amends for his son, as long as there was no scandal, he even offered me something to drink. But the mother went nuts. She lunged at her son, as if to kill him. She shrieked like a rooster. But I was not afraid. I told her, 'My girl is only seventeen and the law is on her side.' She went white and sat down, and shut up, smoothing down her sleeves. The son bent his head and never once looked at me. Only the doctor spoke. He told me for pity's sake to avoid scandal, to consider his position. And he paced the rug up and down. If you could only see the rugs they have. If you could only see the house. It's a beautiful house. They have everything in there."

But I turned my head as though to sleep, so that she'd go away.

In the end I really did fall asleep, and woke up as my father came home. I listened and heard that he was talking to my mother in their room, then, all of a sudden, I heard him shout. "He's going to come and kill me now," I thought. But he didn't come. It was Giovanni who came.

"Nini says why didn't you go pick him up yesterday, and that he'll be waiting for you today," he said.

"I'm in bed, can't you see?" I replied. "I'm sick."

"You probably have scarlet fever," he said. "Everyone has scarlet fever. Azalea's children caught it. Now you too will have a face like a strawberry."

"I don't have scarlet fever," I said. "I have something else."

But he didn't ask what. He looked out the window and said:

"Where is he going?"

I looked out the window and saw my father walking towards town.

"Where is he going? He hasn't even had dinner," Giovanni said.

In the evening Azalea came. She walked into the room with my mother.

"By May we'll have a lovely baby, you know," my mother told her.

She did not reply and sat looking grim, unhooking the fox fur from her shoulders.

"Mammà talks a lot," she told me once we were alone. "It's not at all sure that you'll be married. Papà went there and it was a madhouse, they were at each other's throats. They offered money if Papà kept his mouth shut and you went to have your brat somewhere else, and, as for the wedding, we'll see, we'll see, they said. Papà started shouting that he'd been disgraced, and that he would take them to court if Giulio didn't swear to marry you. He came to me looking ragged. I told you that's how you'd end up. Now you'll have to stay home, because in town they've already started talking. They don't know anything but they can sniff that something's going on. Good for you."

Giovanni came again that evening. Now he, too, had understood and gave me a wicked look. He said:

"Nini still doesn't know about you."

"I don't want you to tell him," I said.

"Don't worry, I won't tell him," he said. "Don't think I get a kick out of talking about the fabulous scrapes you get into. But you got yourself into a proper mess. Who knows whether he'll marry you. He's left meanwhile and no one knows where he is. They say he was already engaged. I don't care. You and your brat can go to hell."

I sat up and threw a glass that was on the night table at him. He started to yell and wanted to hit me but my mother came in. She took him by the collar and dragged him away.

My mother didn't want me to come down to the kitchen or any of the downstairs rooms. for fear that my father might find me in one of them. I found out from Giovanni that my father had sworn that if he happened to see me, he wouldn't come home ever again. But I had no desire to leave my bed. In the morning I'd put on my dress so as to not be cold, slipped on some stockings, and lay back in bed, under a blanket. I felt sick. It got worse with every day. My mother brought me lunch on a tray, but I didn't eat. One evening Giovanni threw a novel at me.

"It's from Nini," he said, "he waited three hours for you outside the factory. He says he's been waiting many days for you. 'She is sick,' I told him."

I tried to read the novel, but then dropped it. Two men killed a girl and locked her up in a trunk. I stopped reading it because it frightened me, and because I wasn't used to reading. After reading for a bit I'd forget what had gone just before. I was not like Nini. My time passed all the same. I had the record player brought to my room, and I listened to the brooding voice sing,

Velvet hands

Perfumed hands

Was it a man or a woman singing? Hard to tell. But I'd become accustomed to that voice, and liked listening to it. I wouldn't have wanted any other song. I didn't want anything new now. I put on the same dress every morning, a worn old dress, darned everywhere. I no longer had any interest in clothes.

When I found myself face to face with Nini, that Sunday morning, while my mother was in church, I was unhappy that he'd come. The flowers dripping rain he held in his hands, his hair wet with rain, his excited smiling face, I looked at all of it as something stupid, something that I didn't know anything about.

"Shut the door," I said in a rage.

"Did I frighten you? Were you sleeping? Here are some flowers," he said coming to sit next to me. "How are you? Are you getting over it? What was it? Your face has become so strange."

"I'm sick," I said. I realized he still didn't know anything.

"Your face has become thin, ugly," he said. "It's bad for you to be cooped up in here. You should go out for a walk. I keep waiting for you in front of the factory. I think, 'Maybe she'll feel well today and come.' Will you come pick me up again when you are well?"

"I don't know."

"Why 'I don't know'? Why that attitude? It's not like you. Tell me if you'll come or won't come any more."

"They don't let me out of the house," I said.

"What do you mean—they don't let you go out?"

"They don't want me to go out with Giulio. Or with you. They don't want me to go out with boys."

"All right," he said, "all right."

He started pacing around the room.

"You're telling me a pack of lies," he said suddenly. "It must be a way you've found to tell me to go to the devil. How you like to see me suffer! How you enjoy it! I can't work, I can't do a thing. All day long I think of you. That's what you wanted, isn't it? That I should poison my life." He looked at me with a mean glint in his eyes. "You've succeeded," he said.

"I couldn't care less about making you suffer," I said and sat up in bed. "Maybe I did like to do that, as you say. But now what do I care? I have other things to think about. I am expecting a child."

"Is that what it is?" he said, and didn't seem surprised. But his voice had gone flat. He put one hand on my shoulder. "Oh you poor girl! Poor girl," he said, "what will you do?"

"I don't know," I replied.

"Will he marry you?"

"I don't know. I don't know anything. But they've talked to him. Maybe he'll marry me, after he finishes his studies."

"You know I love you?"

"Yes," I said.

"Maybe you would have loved me, too, little by little," he said. "But it's no use talking about it now. Talking about it makes it even more painful. It's over. You see, I'm here next to you, but can't find anything more to say to you. I'd like to do something for you, to help you, but at the same time I also feel like just going away and never wanting to hear you mentioned ever again."

"Go then," I said, and started crying.

"I was so happy," he said, "I told myself that little by little you too would fall in love. I thought that sometimes, but sometimes I was afraid of loving you too much. I told myself: 'She'll never love me, she just likes to see people suffer.' What fools we've been, both of us."

We didn't speak for some time. Tears ran down my face.

"Maybe he'll marry me, once he's finished studying," I told him.

"Of course, maybe he'll marry you. And anyway, I'm not right for you. You'd make me suffer too much. We're so different you and I."

He left. I heard his steps on the stairs, I heard him speak to my mother in the orchard. My mother came into my room to say that she'd seen the doctor's family in church, but that Giulio wasn't with them. The doctor had approached her to say that he'd sent Giulio to the city for a while. And then he asked her if he could come and talk to her.

"It's done," my mother said.

The doctor came the same day, and he and my mother withdrew to the dining room and talked for almost two hours. My mother then came upstairs and told me to cheer up, because everyone agreed now, and we'd be married in February. Sooner was not possible because Giulio had to study quietly, without upsets, and we would not see one another till the day of the wedding. In fact, the doctor wanted me to leave town right away, so there wouldn't be any talk. My mother had thought of sending me to my aunt, who lived in a town higher up, not far from ours. My mother was afraid I'd refuse to go. And so she started saying all kinds of nice things to me about that aunt, forgetting that for years they'd been in a dispute over some pieces of furniture. She told me about the vegetable garden my aunt kept in front of her house, a nice big garden where I could stroll as much as I pleased.

"I hate to see you locked up here in this prison. But people are so mean."

Then Azalea came. She and my mother started talking about the day I was to leave, and my mother wanted Azalea to tell her husband to get his company to lend him their car, but Azalea wouldn't hear of it.

I went to my aunt's town in a cart. My mother came with me. We took a side road through the fields so nobody would see me. I wore a coat belonging to Azalea, because my own clothes no longer fit properly and were tight around the waist. We got there at night. My aunt was a very fat woman, with bulging black eyes, who wore a light blue apron and a pair of scissors around her neck since she was a seamstress. She started arguing with my mother over what she should be paid for the time I would be staying with her. My cousin Santa brought me something to eat, lit the fire in the grate, and coming to sit next to me told me that she too was hoping to get married soon, "but I am in no rush," she said laughing loud and long. Her fiancé was the son of the town mayor and they'd been engaged for eight years. He was now doing his military service and sent her postcards.

My aunt's house was large, with vast empty rooms that were all freezing cold. Everywhere were sacks of corn and chestnuts, and onions hung from the ceilings. My aunt had had nine children, but some had died and some had gone away. Only Santa, who was twenty-four and the youngest, remained. My aunt couldn't stand her and yelled at her all day long. If she wasn't married yet it was because my aunt, for one excuse or another, prevented Santa from making up her trousseau.

She liked to keep her at home and torment her without giving her a moment's peace. Santa was afraid of her mother but every time she talked about getting married and leaving her alone she would start to cry. She was surprised that I didn't cry when my mother left. She cried every time her mother went to the city on some business, even though she knew she'd be back by evening. Santa hadn't been to the city more than two or three times. But she said she was happier in her own town. Even though their town was worse than ours. There was a stink of manure, dirty children on the stairs, and nothing more. There was no electricity in the houses and you had to fetch water at the well. I wrote to my mother that I didn't want to stay at my aunt's and that she should come pick me up. She didn't like to write so she didn't reply by mail, but had a man who sold coal tell me to be patient and to stay where I was, because there was no other solution.

So I stayed. I was going to be married in February and it was only November. Ever since I'd told my mother that I was expecting a child my life had become so strange. Ever since then, I'd had to hide like some shameful thing that must not be seen by anybody. I thought of my life the way it had been, of the city I went to every day, of the road to the city, which I had traveled in all seasons, for so many years. I recalled that road so well, the mounds of stones, the hedges, the river one came to suddenly and then the crowded bridge that led to the city's main square. In the city one could buy salted almonds, ice cream. One could look at shop windows, there was Nini leaving the factory, Antonietta scolding the shop salesman, Azalea waiting for her lover and maybe she went to Le Lune with him. But I was far from the city, from Le Lune, from Nini, and was stunned as I thought of all those things. I thought of Giulio, studying in the city, who never wrote to me and never came to see me, as though not remembering me and not knowing he was going to marry me. I thought I had not seen him since he'd found out that we were going to have a child. What did he say? Was he happy or not happy that we were going to be married?

I spent my days sitting in the kitchen at my aunt's house, with the same thoughts always, holding the fire tongs, with the cat on my lap to feel her warmth, and a woolen shawl on my shoulders. Women sometimes came for fittings. My aunt, kneeling, her mouth full of pins, argued over the shape of a neckline and a sleeve and said that when the countess had been alive, she'd had to go to the villa every day to work for her. The countess had died, and my aunt always cried when she mentioned her.

"It was a thrill to feel those silks between one's fingers, those laces," said my aunt. "The poor countess was very fond of me. She'd say, 'My dear Elide, as long as I'm around, you must lack for nothing.'"

But the countess had died in poverty because her children and her husband had squandered all she had.

The women looked at me and were curious and my aunt would tell them that she had taken me in out of pity after my parents had cast me out of the house on account of the misfortune that had befallen me. Some of them wanted to lecture me, but my aunt cut them short:

"What has been has been, and then you never know. Sometimes you think you've made a mistake and then find you did the right thing. Looking at her you might think she's a fool but she's smart, because she's picked a man who is rich and educated who will marry her in the end. It's my daughter who is a fool, making love for eight years and not managing to get herself married. She says it's my fault for not giving her a trousseau. Let them give her a trousseau—they're better off than I am."

"One of these days I'll come home pregnant, then you'll be happy," my cousin would yell at her.

"Just try it, then we'll see," my aunt would say. "I'll tear every tooth out of your mouth if you say that again. No, in my house these kinds of things have never been seen. Out of nine children, five are girls, but as to seriousness no one could ever fault them, because I brought them up properly since they were little. Go ahead, repeat what you just said, you witch," she would tell Santa. Santa would burst out laughing and the women would laugh with her, and my aunt would laugh too, and they kept it up for quite a while.

My aunt was my father's sister. Though she hadn't been to our town for years, and though I'd hardly ever seen her before then, she knew everything about everybody as if she'd always had them around. She didn't like Azalea because she thought her too conceited.

"Who does she think she is, just because she wears a fur in winter," she'd say. "The countess had three furs and she'd throw them into the arms of a servant on entering as if it were any old rag. Though I know what they cost. I know furs pretty well. Azalea's is rabbit. It stinks of rabbit a mile away."

"That Nini is a funny guy," she'd say sometimes. "He is my nephew as much as you are my niece, but I never had a chance to get to know him a little. When I ran into him in the city once, he greeted me warmly and quickly vanished—even though I used to hold him when he was a baby, and I'd sew patches on his trousers because he ran around in tatters. I was told that he is living with a woman."

"He works in a factory," I said.

"Thank God one of you is working. All of my children work, but in your house no one does anything. You've come up like bad weeds, it's a sin even thinking about it. From the moment you came here you've never once made your bed. You spend all day sitting, with your feet up on a stool."

"I'm sick," I'd say. "I'm too sick, I can't tire myself out."

"One can tell how she suffers by just looking at her," Santa said. "She's as green as a lemon, and always pulls a face. Not everyone is as hardy as we are. Because we live among peasants, whereas she grew up close to the city."

"You might as well say she was always in the city, always running away to the city, ever since she was a little kid, and so she has lost all sense of shame. A girl should never set foot in the city, if her mother doesn't go with her. And her own mother was half crazy too. As a young girl, her mother showed no respect either."

"But if Delia gets married she'll be better off than all of us," Santa would say, "and she'll be conceited like Azalea."

"That's true. The day she gets married she won't lack for anything. Let's just see if she gets married. It could go well for her, but who knows. Let's hope."

"When you get married, I'll come be your maid," said Santa after my aunt had left, "if I don't get married too. If I get married I'll have to go work in the fields, with a kerchief on my head and clogs on my feet, sitting on a donkey and sweating, up and down all day. Because my fiancé is a peasant and they have land right next to town, not counting the vineyard, and they keep cows and pigs. I won't be lacking for anything either."

"Oh great. I get sick just thinking about it," I'd say.

"Well, you start feeling sick over nothing," Santa would say, looking offended, as she chopped some cabbage for the soup. "I love Vincenzo and I'd have him even he were poor and in rags, and I had to starve to death with him. Whereas you have no time to think whether you love that man or another, because you have to marry him no matter what, given the condition you're in. And you have to say thank you if he does marry you. I don't mind working if I'm with someone who loves me."

We'd have dinner with a bowl on our knees, without leaving the fire. I never finished my soup. My aunt would pour what remained into her bowl.

"If you go on like this, you'll give birth to a mouse," she'd say.

"It's the darkness that's frightening. It makes me not want to eat. When night falls here it's like being in a tomb."

"Oh poor little thing: you can't eat unless you have electricity. I hadn't heard that one yet. You have to have electricity."

After dinner, Santa and my aunt would stay up late, knitting. They would knit their undershirts. I would get sleepy, but stayed up because I was afraid of going up the stairs by myself. We all slept in the same bed, in the room beneath the attic. In the morning I was the last one to get up. My aunt would go down to feed the chickens, Santa would comb her hair, talking about her fiancé. I slept some and listened some, and told her to polish my shoes. She would polish them watching out for my aunt, because my aunt didn't want me to be catered to. And all the while she went on telling me her tales. She would say, "My name is Santa, but I am no saint." She'd say she was no saint because her fiancé would embrace her when he was back on leave and they would go out together.

Sometimes, I would stroll in the vegetable garden because my aunt said that a pregnant woman mustn't always just sit. She would push me out the door. The vegetable garden was walled in and one could go into town through a wooden gate. But I never opened the gate. I could see the town from the window in our room and there was nothing inviting about it. I walked from the house to the gate, and from the gate to the house. On one end were canes for the tomatoes, on the other were the cabbages. I had to be careful not to trample anything. "Watch out for the cabbages," my aunt would shout, poking her head out the window. The vegetable garden was covered in snow and my feet were frozen. What day was it? What month was it? What were they doing at home? Was Giulio still in the city? I didn't know anything any more. All I knew was that my body was growing, growing, and my aunt had let out my dress twice already. The more my body grew wide and round the more my face became small, ugly, drawn. I always looked at myself in the mirror on the dresser. It was a strange thing, seeing what my face had become. "It's better if no one sees me," I thought. But I was dejected that Giulio hadn't written, and that he had never come to see me.

It was Azalea who came one afternoon. She wore the famous fur and a very odd hat, with three feathers planted at the front of it. Santa was in the kitchen with some little girls, teaching them how to crochet. Azalea looked neither left nor right but took the stairs, and told me she wanted to talk to me face to face. She opened the first door she found, and there was my aunt who had lain down to rest, without her dress and wearing a black slip, her gray braid over her shoulders. When she recognized Azalea she got up all frightened and agitated, and started paying her a thousand compliments as though she couldn't remember all that she had said about her. She wanted to go downstairs and make her some coffee. But Azalea snapped that she didn't want any, and that she wanted to have some time alone with me, because she would be heading back quickly. So my aunt left and we were alone, and she started asking me whether I was feeling very sick.

"You are already quite large," she said. "I think that the day they take you to church you'll be like a balloon."

And she told me that Giulio's father had come offering money again, if only there could be no more talk of weddings. All hell had broken loose at home and he'd gone away frightened, saying that they had misunderstood him and that he was very happy. Then she told me that even after being married I'd have to stay at my aunt's a while longer, till I gave birth, so that there wouldn't be too much talk in our town. And she said that Giulio's mother was an old miser, who did not feed her maid and counted the sheets every day out of fear that someone might steal them, and if I had to go live with her I was not to be envied.

"But Giulio said we'd be by ourselves in the city."

"Let's hope that you can be by yourselves, because if you had to live with her she'll make your life difficult."

"Tell Giovanni to come see me," I told her.

"I'll tell him, but who knows whether he'll come. He's busy with a woman."

"Antonietta?"

"I don't know who she is. She's a blonde Nini used to go out with. They walk arm in arm on the main street. But she is oldish and not a great catch."

"Tell Nini to come see me, too. I'm bored."

"I haven't seen Nini for ages. I'll tell him if I can find him. I'll come see you again but I don't have much time, you know. That man doesn't give me a moment's rest. He always comes whistling beneath my window, and he gestures to me: it's a scandal."

"Is it the student, still?"

"What do you think—that I switch to a new one every month?" she replied offended, pulling on her gloves. "Goodbye," she said, "I'm off," and she hugged me. I was taken by surprise and kissed her cool powdered face. "Goodbye," she repeated on the stairs. I saw her walk stiffly through the vegetable garden, followed by my aunt.

My aunt came to call me to have me try some of her fritters. Everything was still off kilter after Azalea's visit. My aunt told me that she'd asked her if she had any old shoes for Santa and for herself. Azalea had promised to bring some the next time she came. The fritters tasted greasy and made me vomit. Azalea's visit had made me sad. I was sorry I'd told her to ask Nini to come. What effect would I have on him if he did come? I no longer knew myself when I looked in the mirror. I didn't even look like the same person. How I used to run quickly up the stairs once. My step was heavy now, I heard it echo through the house.

Giovanni appeared a few days later. He came on a motorcycle. A friend had lent it to him. As soon as he got off he showed me that he had a watch. And he said he'd bought it with the money he'd made on a commission.

"What's a commission?" I asked.

He explained that someone had commissioned him to sell a pickup truck. Without too much trouble two hundred lira had gone into his pocket.

"It's only imbeciles who break their backs at a factory eight hours a day as Nini does. Money comes into the pocket by itself. You just have to be a good talker. Nini on top of everything is always dead tired—on Sundays he just stays in and sleeps. He's also started drinking worse than before."

"Do you see him often?"

"Not so often. He just moved," he said.

"He is not with Antonietta any more?"

"No."

I wanted to go on asking him about Nini, but he started talking about that money again, about the pickup truck he had sold, and about another commission he was bound to be getting soon, and of a plan he had to buy himself a motorcycle as soon as he had enough money. Santa went out to go to a church function and we remained alone by the fire.

"Do you like it here?" he asked.

"I'm bored," I said.

"Giulio is in the city. Antonietta and I ran into him at the café. He sat with us and bought us something to drink. He said he kills himself studying and has no time to write to you."

"Was Nini there, too?" I asked.

"No—Antonietta and Nini are like a cat and a dog now. Antonietta says that Nini behaved like a heel and went away one morning screaming like a devil. Now he lives alone in one room where he keeps all his books piled up and when he leaves the factory he shuts himself up in there to read and to drink. If I happen to come by he hides the bottle. He doesn't even buy himself food and he is so dirty it's scary. Antonietta gave me some books to take to him that he'd left at her place. 'You can have Antonietta,' he told me. 'Take my place and live with her and you'll be better off than at your house; Antonietta cooks well and makes a fine roast.'"

"So will you go?"

"I'm not stupid," he said. "If I went I'd have to marry her in the end. I'll keep her as long as I like, then I'll break up with her as Nini did. First of all, before she puts on her makeup you can tell how old she is. And she's always whining about something that's a bore to listen to."

He stayed for dinner and frightened Santa with the story of a ghost that popped up on the road at night. I stepped out with him into the vegetable garden.

"Goodbye," he said, getting up onto the seat of the motorbike. "Keep your spirits up. When you no longer have that watermelon in your belly, I'll take you to the movies with Antonietta. You see amazing things at the movies. I go often because Antonietta knows the owner and they let us in on a discount."

He left making a big din, with smoke coming out the back of his cycle.

My aunt and Santa were still talking about the ghost: they talked about it all evening and they also talked about a nun who always appeared at the fountain and whom Santa had seen once, and even I started to be afraid. In bed I couldn't fall asleep and couldn't stop thinking about the nun, and I tried to wake Santa up by pulling on her arm, but she turned the other way muttering something. I got up and walked barefoot to the window and thought of Nini, drinking in his room, with his ruffled lock of hair, and putting the bottle away quickly when Giovanni came. I felt an urge to speak to Nini—to tell him that I was afraid of the nun and of ghosts, and to hear him laughing and making fun of me as he used to do. But could he still laugh? Maybe he didn't laugh any more, maybe he'd gone kind of mad with drink. I felt like crying, and started to cry and shout standing upright in the room in my nightgown with my hands on my face. My aunt woke up and leapt out of bed, lit a candle and asked me what was the matter. She told me not to be silly, to get back into bed, and go to sleep.

Santa's boyfriend came on leave—a tall man with a terracotta-colored face, who was too shy to speak. Santa asked me if I liked her boyfriend.

"No," I said.

"Maybe you only like men with mustaches," she said.

"No," I said, "I also like some who don't have a mustache." And I thought of Nini and again wanted to be with him, far from Santa and from my aunt, stretched out by the side of the river in the light blue dress I wore all summer. I would have liked to know whether he still loved me as much. But I was so ugly and weird-looking now that I would have been ashamed to show myself to him. Even with Santa's boyfriend I was ashamed.

Santa was mad at me for telling her I didn't like her boyfriend. She didn't talk to me for several days, till I had to call her over and apologize once when I needed her to help me wash my hair. She heated the water and brought it to me, and she kissed me and was moved, and told me that when I went away she would find it hard to get used to being without me. And she wanted me to promise that I would write to her sometimes.

There was a little bit of sun so I sat out in the vegetable garden to let my hair dry, with a towel over my shoulders. All at once I saw the gate open and Nini walked in.

"How are you?" he asked. He was the same as ever, with the raincoat and the crooked hat, and a scarf flung around his neck, but he seemed distracted and unfriendly and I couldn't think of anything to say. And then I was too upset that he should see what I had become. He said we should leave the garden and take a walk outside because he didn't feel like talking to my aunt. I took the towel off and followed him out, and we walked for a long while through the bare vines, on cold icy snow.

"How are you?" I said.

"Not well," he answered. "Are you getting married in February?"

"Yes, in February."

"Does Giulio come here often?"

"No. He never came."

"Are you sorry that he never comes?"

I didn't answer and he stopped in front of me, looking straight into my eyes.

"No, you are not sorry. You don't give a damn even about him. That should make me happy. But it hurts even more. It's such a stupid story, if you think about it—it shouldn't be worth agonizing over any more."

He stopped again, waiting for me to say something.

"Did you know that I'm living alone now?"

"Yes, I know."

"I like living alone. I spend whole days without saying a word to anyone. I get out of the factory and immediately go to my room where I have my books and no one can bother me."

"Is it a nice room?" I asked.

"Not at all."

I slipped and he caught me by the arm.

"Maybe you'd like to know if I'm still in love with you. No, I don't think I'm in love any more."

"That's good," I said. But it wasn't true and I felt so sad I was having a tough time not crying.

"When I came to see you last time, and they told me you were sick, I wanted to ask you to marry me. I don't know how I got that absurd notion. You would certainly have said no, or laughed, or gotten angry, but I wouldn't have suffered so much. What made me suffer was to know that you will have a child, that you with that face, that hair, that voice, will have a child that you may even love, and that maybe little by little you will turn into someone else, and what will I be to you then? My life won't change, I will go on working at the factory and bathing in the river in the summer and reading my books. Once I used to be happy always, I liked looking at women, I liked going around the city and buying books, all the while thinking about many things, and I felt intelligent. I would have liked us to have a child together. But I never even told you how much I loved you. I was afraid of you. What a stupid story it's been. It's useless to cry," he said, seeing the tears in my eyes. "Don't cry. It makes me angry to see you cry. I know you don't care. You cry now, but what do you really care?"

"You, too, no longer care about me now," I told him.

"No," he answered. It was getting dark. He walked me back to the gate.

"Goodbye," he said. "Why did you have them ask me to come here?"

"Because I wanted to see you."

"You wanted to see what I have become? I'm in perfect shape," he said, "all I do is drink."

"Well you always did drink."

"Not like now. Goodbye. I didn't tell you the truth. I said I didn't love you any more. That's not true, I still love you."

"Even though I'm so ugly now?" I asked him.

"Yes," he said, and laughed. "You really have become ugly. Goodbye, I'm going."

"Goodbye," I said.

I found Santa crying in the kitchen, because Vincenzo

had told her as he left that his family wouldn't allow them to marry. They wanted another girl who had some money. He had promised to marry her anyway, but my aunt said that he would never make up his mind. My aunt asked where I'd been. I said I'd gone walking with Nini.

"Oh, Nini. He could have come say hello to me. I saw his mother die."

Santa didn't want any dinner.

"You're really stupid," my aunt told her, "what's all the rush to get married? Here at home you have all you need. When a woman gets married all her troubles begin. The children are crying, the husband wants to be served, the in-laws make life difficult. If you had taken Vincenzo you would have had to go into the fields early in the morning, to dig and mow, because they are peasants. You would have found out how nice that is. A girl doesn't understand life. What could be better for you than to stay at home with your mother?"

"Yes, but what about later?" Santa answered, sobbing.

"Later? Later, you mean as when I'll be dead? Are you in such a hurry to see me die? I'll live to ninety just to spite you," shouted my aunt, hitting her on the head with her rosary.

"Your cousin is different," she went on after a bit, as Santa dried her tears. "She had a bad mishap. Did you play me some dirty trick too?"

"No, I swear."

"I sure hope so. In my house these kinds of things never happened. But sometimes a bad example is like rotten fruit. If Delia had been my daughter I would have given her a couple of slaps this evening One doesn't go around with a young man in the condition you're in," she told me, "as you did today with Nini. It doesn't matter that you grew up together. Not everyone knows that."

I didn't answer and started comforting Santa instead. I said:

"Don't despair. After I'm married I'll find you a husband, too."

"Come now," my aunt said, "you're in no position to declare victory yet. I heard that your fiancé has no intention of marrying you and is going out with some young lady. More than one person told me that and I believe it. Why else wouldn't he come to see you—everyone has come, even that crazy Nini, so why didn't he come?"

"Well he has to study," I said.

" I don't know. I'm just repeating what I heard. They see him with a young lady, that's what I was told. You're a simpleton to stay here waiting for him to come marry you, when he can't even remember who you are."

"That's not true," I said.

"Why don't you go ask him if it's true. Stand up for yourself a little and tell him he has to marry you, now that he has ruined you, and that otherwise you'll make a scandal. Men must be ruled by fear. It will be nice when you have a child on your arm and you have to make a living. Because your father won't take you back home, I can tell you that."

She left and I was alone with Santa. Santa said:

"How miserable we are," and she wanted to hold me

close so that we could cry together, but I didn't want her near me. I fled to the room upstairs and locked the door.

I didn't cry but looked dumbly into the dark, thinking he was right not to want to marry me. Because I'd become ugly now, Nini had said so, too, and anyway I didn't love him, I couldn't care less about him. "It would be better if I died," I thought, "I've been too stupid and unlucky. I don't even know what I want now." But maybe the only thing I wanted was to go back to being what I'd been before, to put on my light blue dress and take off to the city every day, and look for Nini and see if he was in love with me, and also to go into the woods with Giulio only without marrying him. But all that was over and could never be again. And when my life had been like that, I couldn't stop thinking that I was bored and waiting for something else to happen, and hoping that Giulio would marry me so I could leave home. Now I no longer wanted to marry him and remembered how often I had been bored while he talked to me, and how often he'd been mean to me. "But it's useless," I thought, "it's useless and we have to get married, and if he won't have me I'll be ruined forever."

The next day my mother came and found I had a fever, thanks to having hung around in the cold with Nini till late in the evening, my aunt told her. The room was too cold and I sat in the kitchen in my usual spot, with my legs practically in the fire. My teeth were chattering and I complained about the fever I felt on me. My head was muddled and I couldn't quite understand what my mother was saying. My mother was saying that there had been another scene between Giulio and my father, because Giulio had said that the child might not even be his.

"If you hadn't always been a good-for-nothing you wouldn't have heard such words spoken," my mother told me.

"It's true," said my aunt, "and just yesterday she went out walking with Nini, and that's why she got a fever, from the chill she got. I don't care, but I am sorry to have her staying here with us. Because if her bad reputation sticks to my daughter, how will we ever get rid of it?"

But I told them to go away and leave me alone because my bones ached. My aunt told my mother that I should speak to Giulio, if he was the one who didn't want me, and my mother also thought that I should speak to him, and left me his address in the city, which she had secretly gotten from the maid. Then she went on her way quickly so that she could be home before my father got back, because my father didn't want her to come see me and said that even if I were to die he didn't want to hear about it.

And so one day, when I had recovered, I got ready to go to the city, took the money my mother had left me and a parcel of sweets my aunt had made which she wanted me to take to Giulio, though I gave the sweets to a woman when I got on the bus. The whole time I was on the bus I couldn't stop thinking about the city, which I hadn't seen in a long time, and also liked looking out the window and looking at the people getting on and listening to what they were saying. It was definitely more interesting than the kitchen, because sad thoughts went away when there were so many people who didn't know me and didn't know my story. It cheered me up to see the city, with the porticoes and the main street, and I looked to see if by any chance Nini might be there, but at that hour he was probably at the factory. I bought some stockings and a perfume called "Nocturne," till I had no money left. Then I went to Giulio's. The landlady, who had a mustache, and walked dragging one leg, told me he was sleeping and that she didn't dare wake him, but that if I waited a bit he would be getting up. She led me into the drawing room and opened the shutters, and sat with me and started to tell me about her leg, how it had swelled after she'd fallen down the stairs, and she told me about the treatments she was having and the money it was costing. When she went to open the door to the milkman I quickly removed my stockings and put on the new ones I had bought, and rolled up the ones with runs in them and put them in my bag. Then I sat down again and waited till the landlady came to call me, and I found Giulio in his room, so sleepy he didn't know who I was. Then he started walking around barefoot looking for his tie and jacket, while I leafed though his books on the table, but he told me to stop and not to touch anything.

"Who knows why you came here," he told me. "I'm busy and really don't like wasting time. And then what will they say here, I'll have to explain who you are."

"You'll say that we are going to be married," I told him, "or don't you want to get married any more?"

"Are you afraid I'll run away?" he said in a rage. "Don't worry, I won't get away from you now."

"Listen," I said in a low quiet voice that didn't feel like my own, "I know you no longer care for me. And I no longer care for you. But as for marrying, you have to marry me, because otherwise I'll throw myself into the river."

"Oh," he said, "you read that in some novel."

But he was a bit frightened and, telling me not to repeat such rubbish, he shouted to the landlady to make us some coffee. After I'd had the coffee, he took the cups away, then shut the door and locked it, and told me that instead of talking there was a better way to spend our time.

When I saw out the window that it was dark I said that my bus had already left, and then he looked at his watch and told me to get dressed quickly, that maybe I could still catch it.

"Or where would I put you tonight?" he said. "There's no way I can keep you here, or the lame woman will go telling the whole town about it."

He got cross with me at the bus stop because I couldn't find my ticket, then because in the rush the contents of my handbag spilled and the old stockings I had removed in the drawing room came tumbling out, and he said:

"You really haven't changed. You'll never learn how to live."

The night before my wedding I couldn't stop crying, and my aunt made me spend two hours with cold compresses on my face, so it wouldn't show too much. Then she washed my hair with egg yolk and spread cream on my hands which were red and cracked. It was the cream the countess had always used. But whenever anyone spoke to me I cried, and I was a sorry sight, with my just-washed hair flying in every direction, my eyes swollen from crying, and my trembling mouth.

In the morning my father and mother came on a cart, and after a while the two little ones came walking, hoping to eat something. But they were so dirty that my aunt didn't allow them to come to the church. They hadn't found Giovanni because he had already gone to the city, and told me Azalea was at the seaside with her children who were recovering from an illness. She had written me a letter in which she explained that she was there with her lover and didn't feel like leaving. Later, Giulio and his father came. Giulio was unrecognizable in his long raincoat, the gloves he held in one hand, and his polished shoes. My aunt borrowed some chairs, because the straw on hers had thinned.

In church I understood not one word that the priest was saying. I was dead scared that all of a sudden I'd feel ill from the pounding of my heart and the smell of incense. The church had just been repainted and was so bare and empty that it hardly looked like a church. My mother had brought a small heater along and my aunt kept glancing at the door, worrying about the lunch she had on the stove. Santa cried out of grief that she was not the one getting married, and I was crying too and couldn't stop. I cried all through the lunch my aunt had prepared. But the others pretended not to notice me and started talking among themselves about things that didn't concern me.

When my father got up to leave, my aunt pushed me to go to him and told me to ask forgiveness for the sorrow I had caused him. He was embarrassed as he kissed me and turned his head away. He had changed a great deal in those months and now wore an expression that was permanently offended and sad. He wore glasses and didn't even look like the same person who had beaten me about Giulio. It seemed that all desire for beatings, shouting, and getting angry had left him. He looked at me on the sly and never said a word. He seemed ashamed of me.

After lunch everyone except Giulio left. We went up to the room and he told me I'd have to stay with my aunt till the baby was born. He would come see me now and then, but not too often. Because he had tired himself out studying, and I had to keep calm, too, because giving birth is no joke. He told me to lie down and rest after all that I had been through in church, and he left me and went down to the kitchen with Santa who was drying the glasses.

He came to see me one Sunday. He was once again

dressed to go hunting, wearing black boots and his jacket unbuttoned, as he looked when I'd run into him in town. I asked him whether he had already found us some lodgings.

"What lodgings?" he asked. "We won't be needing any lodgings—we'll be living with my parents, my mother has already gotten our room ready."

"Oh really?" I replied, and my voice shook with rage. "But I don't want to live with your mother. I'd rather die than to see your mother every day."

"I won't allow you to talk like that," he said. And he said that soon he'd have a studio in the city, but that I had to live in town with his parents because the cost of living was too high and we didn't have the means to live by ourselves.

"It would have been better not to get married then," I said.

"Of course it would have been better," he said. "But I married you because I felt sorry for you. Have you already forgotten that you wanted to jump in the river?"

I looked him square in the face and left. I crossed the vegetable garden quickly without saying anything to my aunt who asked where the devil I was going. I started walking through the vines as I had done that day with Nini, and walked at length with my hands in my pockets and the wind blowing in my face. When I got back Giulio had left.

"You swine," my aunt said, "you really know how to earn some respect. I was just going by and heard you arguing—it's a bit too soon for that. You're going to really put him through it if you go on like that."

Giulio came back after a few days with some fabric lengths, because he wanted me to have new clothes made up, and he told me he would think some more about the business of living in the city.

"I am angering my parents just to please you, but you don't deserve anything, because you're too mean."

My aunt came to look at the fabrics and pulled out a fashion magazine, and said that the minute I had the child she would get to work. But Giulio said that he would bring the fabrics to a seamstress in the city. Offended, my aunt went red in the face and told us to leave the room and go down to the kitchen because she had to straighten out a closet. "And after all, this is my house," she said.

Giulio told me that I had to be elegant if I wanted to live in the city. But he said that he wouldn't let me dress the way Azalea did. Because Azalea wore some extravagant things and when she went by people in the street stopped to stare at her. He didn't want that to happen to me. But as for being stylish he did want me to be stylish because when a woman neglects herself it's no fun being seen with her. Just to spite him, Santa told him that he had made a bad choice with the fabrics, because those weren't the fashionable colors.

"People who spend their life among onions really know about fashion," Giulio said.

"Fashion is to dress like everyone else, not with ogre boots like yours that make me laugh the minute I lay eyes on them," Santa replied.

They were both offended and Giulio went on talking to me as if he were alone in the room with me. He told me that if we lived in the city we'd have to have people over now and then, and I'd have to learn to do that and many other things, because sometimes you'd think I had fallen off the face of the moon. I looked at him wondering if he was thinking of Le Lune as he said that. But he wasn't thinking about that at all and it was as though he didn't even remember that he had taken me to Le Lune, where whores also went, it seemed he no longer remembered the time when we hadn't been married, when he'd hardly wanted to marry me, and when I should have accepted the money to go get lost somewhere, along with the child I had with him. Now he often talked about our child, about the face he imagined the child would have, and of a new type of collapsible pram he had seen that we should buy.

My labor started at night. My aunt got up and called the midwife, and sent Santa to her godmother because she said that a young girl shouldn't see how a baby is born. But Santa wanted to stay because she couldn't wait to kiss the child and put the bonnet with light blue ribbons she had embroidered for him on his head. Toward morning my mother came, also bearing bonnets with ribbons. But I was distraught from the pain and the fear: I had already fainted twice and the midwife said I had to be taken to the city hospital right away.

While the car sped toward the city, and my mother watched me crying, I looked at my mother's face thinking I would soon be dead. I dug my nails into my mother's hands and shrieked.

I gave birth to a boy and he was immediately baptized, because it looked as though he would die. But the next morning he was fine. I was weak and had a fever, and was told not to breastfeed him. I spent one month at the hospital after the baby was born. The nuns looked after my baby, and they fed him with a bottle. Every now and then, they would bring him to me—ugly as sin in the bonnet embroidered by Santa—his long fingers moving slowly, very slowly, and with a mysterious fixed gaze as though he were about to come upon something.

The day after the birth my mother-in-law came to see me and she immediately picked on a nun saying the swaddling of the baby was badly done. Then she sat stiffly, handbag in hand, her face long and sad, and told me that when she had given birth she had suffered far more than I had. The doctors had praised her courage. And, in spite of the doctors' opinion, she had insisted on breastfeeding the baby. She said she had cried all day when she had found out that I wouldn't be breastfeeding. She searched through her handbag for a handkerchief and dried her tears.

"It is sad when a baby is denied the mother's breast," she said. But added that I didn't have good breasts. She came to inspect them under my nightshirt. With breasts like those I couldn't breastfeed. I lost my temper and told her I wanted to sleep, because I was tired and my head ached. So she asked me if I was offended and stroked my chin, and said that she was perhaps a bit too outspoken. She pulled out a box of dates and slipped them under my pillow.

"Call me Mamma," she said on leaving.

After she left, I ate all the dates, one by one, and put the box back thinking it might be useful to keep my gloves in. And I started thinking about a certain pair of gloves I'd buy when I left the hospital—white leather ones with black stitching, like Azalea's, and then of all the dresses and hats I'd buy, to be elegant and spite my mother-in-law, who would say that I was wasting money. But I was sad, both because my mother-in-law had come and now I knew for sure that I'd have her around all the time, and because it seemed to me that the baby looked like her. When they had brought the baby to me and put him next to me in bed, I told myself that he looked like her and that that was why I didn't love him. It made me sad to have brought that baby into the world, with a chin as long as my mother-in-law's, a baby who also looked like Giulio, but in no way like me. "If I loved Giulio, I'd have loved the baby, too," I thought, "but the way things are I just can't." Still, there was something about his limp damp hair, his body, and way of breathing that stayed with me when they took him away. It didn't matter to him to know whether I loved him, whether I was sad or happy, what I wanted to buy, or the thoughts I had, and I felt sorry to see how tiny and stupid he still was, because it would have been better if I could have talked to him. He sneezed and I covered him with my shawl. And I was startled recalling that I'd had him in me, he had lived beneath my dress for such a long time, while I sat with my aunt in the kitchen, and when Nini came and we had walked in the garden. Why had Nini not come to visit me? But it was better that he didn't come yet because I was far too tired and weak, and every time I made an effort to speak my head ached. And then he would have said something mean about the baby.

Giulio always came to see me toward evening, when the nuns prayed in the hallway and a small lamp under a silk shade was lit by my bedside. When he came, I started complaining right away that I didn't feel well, that my whole body ached as if I'd been beaten and stepped on, which was true, but I enjoyed scaring him. Then I'd say I was sick of being at the hospital, that the hours never passed, and I told him that one day I'd slip out and go to the movies. Then he would beg me to be patient, and comforted me, and promised, if I didn't drive him to despair, to bring me a present. He was tender to me now and told me he'd do anything to make me happy, and had already rented an apartment in the city, with an elevator and all that we needed.

It wasn't true that I didn't like being at the hospital, I liked it because I didn't have to do anything, whereas the moment I left I'd have to rock the baby and get his milk ready, and wash his bottom every other minute. Now I didn't even really know how to swaddle him, and was afraid when he cried because he would go purple in the face and look as if he might burst. But sometimes I was fed up with not being able to get out of bed and look at myself in the mirror and put on some clothes, and go out and see the city, now that I had some money. There were days when I couldn't get rid of the boredom, then I'd wait for someone to turn up. My mother hardly ever came because she was busy, and because she was too badly dressed to be seen in the city. She was no longer as happy about my marriage, and had argued with Giulio when she'd asked him to lend her some money and he'd said no. My mother hadn't forgiven him and sulked even with me.

One day Azalea, who had just returned from the seaside, came to see me, in sandals and with her nose peeling. But she was sad because things weren't going well with her lover now—he was madly jealous and didn't want her to go dancing, and they fought all day long.

"How is your son?" she asked.

I asked if she wanted to see him, but she said she'd had her fill with her own children and that when they were that tiny she'd found them repellent.

"How's it going with your husband?" she asked. "You were right not to let him have his way because if you'd gone to live with his mother it would have been all over and you'd never have seen a cent. You must always do as you please with men, because if you act like a weakling, they'll take away the very air you breathe."

The next day she brought me her seamstress, though I had told her that my measurements couldn't be taken yet since I wasn't supposed to get out of bed. But Azalea reassured me that the seamstress would come just to get to know me and talk to me about current fashions. Then she began to insist I get up, saying I was well enough by now, and was in much better shape than she was.

When I got up the first time and slipped on a pink dressing gown with a swan on it Azalea had brought, I felt happy, and walking very slowly with Giulio in the hospital hallway, I looked out the tall windows overlooking the main street. Nini might have been going by just then. I sat by the window and watched in case he did, because I would have called out to him , to tell him to come see me, and we would have started bickering and talking. He certainly didn't love me any more now, after so much time had gone by, and even if he did still love me it didn't seem right that we should stop seeing each other. But I didn't see him go by and it made me sad, and I argued with the nuns because they wanted me to go back to bed.

It was Giovanni who told me the truth when he came to see me bringing a little trumpet to give to the baby as though he might already be able to play it. He held a leather briefcase in one hand and said that he now worked as a textile salesman, and traveled around showing his fabrics. But his face looked worn and frightened as if he had come out of some bad business, and he talked waving his arms as though he were hiding something from me. "Antonietta must have left him," I thought. I asked him what had happened.

"Nothing," he replied. But he kept on walking, waving his hands, and all of a sudden stopped before the wall, keeping his back to me. He said, "Nini has died.'

I put down the baby I'd been holding in my arms.

"Yes, he died," he said, and started crying, and I fell, sitting, limp, and short of breath. He calmed down little by little, and dried his face, and said that they had warned him that I shouldn't be told, because I wasn't well yet, but many days had gone by since he had died. Of pneumonia. But Antonietta said it was my fault. She said I was too hard-hearted, because Nini had been in love with me for a long time, even while still living with her, and I had tortured him so, and went looking for him even when I'd known I was pregnant and would be getting married. He'd lost his wits then and had started living like a tramp, in a room that was a cesspool, without sleeping or eating, and all the time getting drunk. Antonietta said that if she ever ran into me, she would shame me in front of everyone. But Giovanni said there was no truth to what she said, because Nini was too cold, he wasn't interested in women, all he wanted to do was drink. But when he'd found him ranting in bed, he'd assumed he was drunk and had poured a pitcher of water on him, which Antonietta said had made him even sicker. Because Giovanni had gone to fetch Antonietta, and Antonietta had said right away that it looked like pneumonia. They had gone in search of a doctor and for three days they had put poultices on his back, as the doctor had ordered, and she had cleaned the room and brought some blankets from her place. But he was breathing hard and never stopped ranting, and he kept trying to heave himself off the bed—they had to forcefully restrain him—until he died.

That evening when Giulio came he found me crying, crying and pacing around the room, and I didn't want to go back to bed. On the table was the tray the nun had brought, with the soup grown cold in the plate, that I hadn't touched.

"What happened?" he asked.

"Nini died," I said, "Giovanni told me."

"That pig Giovanni," he said, "when I see him I'll smash his face."

He took my wrist and said I had a fever, and begged me to go back to bed. But I didn't answer and went on crying, and he said he was ashamed that the nuns should see me that way, half-naked as I was, my dressing gown open down the front, and did I also want to catch pneumonia and go to the next world like Nini. He was offended and phoned Azalea to come, and started reading the paper without looking at me.

Azalea came and told him to go have dinner at the restaurant, so he went and said he would leave us alone with our secrets, since he didn't count, and wasn't needed.

"He's jealous," Azalea said after he'd left, "they're all jealous."

"Nini died," I told her.

"That's no news," she said. "He died. I cried too when they told me. Then I thought it was better like that for him. I hope it'll happen to me, too, soon. I'm fed up with living."

"It's my fault that he died," I told her.

"Your fault?"

"Because he loved me," I said, "and I tortured him and I liked to watch him suffer, till he started drinking more than before, and spending all his time alone in a room, and not caring about anything any more after he found out I was getting married."

But Azalea looked at me in disbelief and said spitefully:

"When someone dies one gets ideas into one's head. He died because he got sick, and you can't do anything about it and it's useless for you to embroider the facts. He couldn't care less about you—he always said you were silly and didn't know how to turn men down, and that he felt sorry for you."

"He loved me," I said. "He always took me down to the river to talk. He read his books to me and explained what they meant. He kissed me once. And I loved him, too. But I didn't know it and I thought I just liked to have fun with him."

"There's no point in your dreaming about Nini now," she said. "Nini or someone else, it's all the same. Just as long as you have someone because life is too sad for a woman if she is by herself. Nini was a bit less stupid than the others, it's true, and he had sparkling eyes—you can still feel them on your skin—but after a while you'd get weary of him, you never knew what he was thinking. I am not surprised that he died, wasted with grappa as he was, it's surprising he didn't die sooner."

That night I dreamed that Nini had come to the hospital, secretly taken the baby, and gone away, but I ran after him and asked him where he'd put the baby, and he pulled it out from inside his jacket, but the baby had become very very small, the size of an apple, and all of a sudden Nini ran off, up a staircase, and Giovanni was there, too, and I called to him but he didn't answer.

I woke up perspiring and in a frenzy and saw Giulio by my bed, because it was morning, and he had come early to see how I was feeling. I told him I had dreamed that Nini had stolen the baby.

"No, he hasn't been stolen," he said. "He's there, sleeping—don't be afraid, no one is going to come and steal him."

But I kept on telling him that Nini had appeared before my eyes as if he were alive, that he had touched me and talked to me, and I sobbed and tossed about on the bed. He told me to try to control myself and not to be so nervous.

A few days later, I left the hospital and went to live in my new house. And another life began for me, a life in which there was no Nini, who had died and whom I no longer was to think about since it was pointless; there was the baby was instead, and Giulio, and the house with new furniture and curtains and lamps, and a maid my mother-in-law had unearthed, and my mother-in-law who came now and then. The maid took care of the baby and I slept late every morning, in the large double bed, with the orange velvet bedspread, with a rug to put one's feet on, and a bell to call the maid. I would get up and walk around the house in my dressing gown, and admire the furniture and the rooms, brushing my hair deliberately, slowly, and sipping coffee. I thought of my mother's house, with chicken shit everywhere, with damp stains on the walls, with small paper flags attached to the lamp in the dining room. Did that house still exist? Azalea said we should go there together one day, but I didn't feel like going there because I was ashamed to think that I had lived there once, and then I would have been pained to see Giovanni's room, where Nini had also slept when we were all living together. When I went out in the city I stayed away from the river, and looked for the most crowded streets so as to be seen by people, as I was now, in my new clothes, wearing lipstick. I felt so beautiful now that I never tired of looking at myself in the mirror, and it seemed to me that no woman had ever been so beautiful.

When my mother-in-law came, she would closet herself in the kitchen with the maid, and I would put my ear to the door and listen. The maid would say that I didn't love the baby, that I never picked him up when he cried, I never even asked whether he had eaten, and she had to do everything, take care of the baby and cook and clean, because I was always out walking, looking at myself in the mirror or sleeping, and didn't even know how to make broth. My mother-in-law would complain to Giulio, but he would say it wasn't true, that I doted on the baby and that he saw me cradling him all the time, and if I went for a walk now and then he saw no harm in it, because I was young and I had to have some distractions, and he was the one who encouraged me to go out. Giulio was now so in love with me he no longer cared about his mother or anyone else, and his mother was always saying that he had gone stupid and no longer saw the truth, and if one day I cuckolded him, he would have gotten what he deserved. But she never said anything to me because she was afraid of me, and she always smiled when she spoke to me and invited me to come visit her, and never again dared to open my drawers after I had told her to mind her own business.

"When the baby is older, " I thought, "it will be more fun, when he starts running around the house on a tricycle, when I start having to buy him toys and candy." But now he was always the same every time I looked at him, his large head resting on the pillow in his cradle, and after a while a kind of rage came over me and I had to get away. I couldn't believe that I could go out and have the city all to myself, without having had to walk a long time on a dusty road full of carts, and be disheveled and tired when I got there, upset at the thought that I'd have to leave again at sundown when it became even more interesting. I would meet Azalea and we would go sit in a café. Little by little I started to live like Azalea. I spent my days in bed and got up toward evening, made up my face and went out, with a fox fur over one shoulder. As I walked, I'd look around and smile impertinently, as Azalea always did.

On my way home once I ran into Antonietta and Giovanni. They walked arm in arm, their backs bent since it was raining and they didn't have an umbrella. "Hello," I said. We went to a café together. I expected Antonietta to suddenly pounce on me and scratch me with her sharp polished nails, which she must have spent whole days manicuring, though it was hardly worth it, given how old and ugly she had become. But she didn't seem to want to scratch me, she looked almost afraid of what I might say about her, and hid her feet behind an armchair, when she saw me looking at them. She said she had seen my baby in the pram, on an outing in the park, and would have liked to approach to give him a little kiss, but hadn't dared on account of the maid.

"Lucky you to have a maid," she told me, "I have to do everything myself. But I don't have much to do since there are no men in the house, I am alone with the children."

After saying that she blushed, and red blotches appeared on her neck, and we stopped talking and just
looked at one another, with the same thought in our
head. But she started asking me about the baby again
and about my husband, and whether I went dancing
and led a "fun life."

"You never come home," Giovanni told me, and said
that at home it was the same old story, and I was lucky
to have gotten away. He asked to borrow some money,
because though he worked they took everything at
home and his pockets were always empty.

They walked me to my front door and there we
said goodbye, and while I undressed in the bedroom,
I thought of Giovanni who might now be crossing the
bridge to go home on the dark road, because he didn't
want to stay with Antonietta, otherwise he'd have to
marry her. We never said a word about Nini the entire
time we were at the café together, as if we'd forgotten
that he, too, used to like to sit at that café, smoking and
talking, sprawled sideways on the chair, with his hands
in his lock of hair and his chin raised. But it became
harder and harder to think of him, of his face, and of
the things he said, and to me he seemed so far away
that it was scary thinking about it—because the dead
are scary.

AFTERWORD

I started writing *The Road to the City* in September, 1941. September was wafting about in my head, a countryside September in the Abruzzo region that is not rainy but warm and peaceful, with the earth turning red, the hills turning red, and a nostalgia for Turin was also floating about in my head, and maybe also *Tobacco Road*, which I had, I think, just read and liked somewhat—not too much. And all those things combined in me. I felt like writing a novel, not just a short story. But I didn't know whether I'd have enough breath for it.

When I started to write I was once again afraid it would only be a short story. I was also afraid that it would be too long and tedious. And I remembered how my mother, whenever she read a novel that was too long and tedious, would say, "What a blathering bore!" I had never before thought of my mother while writing. And if I had thought of her, I always felt I couldn't care less what her opinion might be. But my mother was far away now and I missed her. For the first time, I felt the impulse to write something that my mother might like.

So, to avoid blathering, I wrote and rewrote the first few pages, trying to be as dry and spare as possible. I wanted every sentence to be like a slap or the lash of a whip.

Real characters, uninvited, started entering the story I had thought up. I am not sure however that I had ac-

tually thought of a story. I found out that you have to
have a short story in your head as though in a shell, but
that a long story at one point begins to unwind all on
its own, almost *writing itself*. I had lingered at length
over the first few pages, but once they were done, I had
a running start and kept going in a single breath.

My characters were people of the village—people I
saw from the window or encountered coming and going.
Unbid and unwanted they came into the story: I recognized some of them right away; others I recognized
only once I'd finished writing. But blended into them,
and just as unwittingly, were friends and my closest
relatives. And the road—the road that cut the town in
half and ran through hills and fields all the way to the
city of Aquila—had also entered the story which didn't
yet have a title, and though for years I'd had titles in my
head, now that I was writing a novel I had no idea what
title to give it. When I'd finished my novel (that's what I
called it to myself), I counted the characters and found
that there were twelve. Twelve! This seemed like a lot
to me. All the same, I despaired because what I had was
not a novel but nothing more than a fairly long story.
I don't know whether I liked it. Or rather, I liked it to
an unbelievable degree because it was mine, yet in the
end worrying that it was not saying anything special.

The road was, then, the road mentioned. The city was
both Aquila and Turin. The town was the beloved ab-
horred town I'd been living in for over a year and which
I now knew down to its remotest alleys and trails. The
girl who says "I" was a girl I always used to run into on

those paths. The house was her house and the mother was her mother. But she was to some degree also an old school friend of mine, one I hadn't seen in years. Partly she was also, in an obscure and confused way, I myself. And from then on, whenever I used the first person, I found that I myself, unbid, and unwanted, slipped into my writing.

I gave no name either to the town or to the city. I had an old aversion to using the names of actual places. And found using names of invented places repellent (though I did so later on). Likewise, I had a profound aversion to last names and it took me years to free myself of that aversion: I don't think I am free of it even now.

When I finished that novel, I found that if there was anything alive in it, it grew out of bonds of love and hate that tied me to that town; and it grew out of the hate and the love through which the inhabitants of the town as well as my relatives, friends, and brothers had teamed up and mixed: and I said to myself once more that I shouldn't write about anything foreign or indifferent to me, and that my characters should always conceal real people closely linked to me. It seems that while I did not have intimate ties to the people of the town, those I encountered in passing and who had entered my story, I did have close ties of love and hate to the town as a whole—and my friends and brothers had become en-meshed with the inhabitants of the town. And I decided that that meant writing not *accidentally*. To write *accidentally* was to let oneself go to the game of pure obser-vation and invention, which moves beyond us, picking at random among beings, places, and things to which we are indifferent. To write not accidentally is to write only about what we love. Memory is loving and never *accidental*. It sinks its roots in our very life, and so its choices are never *accidental*, but always impassioned and imperious. I thought all that, then I forgot all about it, and then for many years I gave myself over to the game of idle invention, believing I could invent from nothing, without love or hate, playing among beings and things for whom I felt nothing but an idle curiosity.

It wasn't I who found the title, *The Road to the City*. It was my husband. The book came out in 1942 under a pseudonym, and in that town, no one ever found out that I had written and printed a book.

NATALIA GINZBURG, 1964